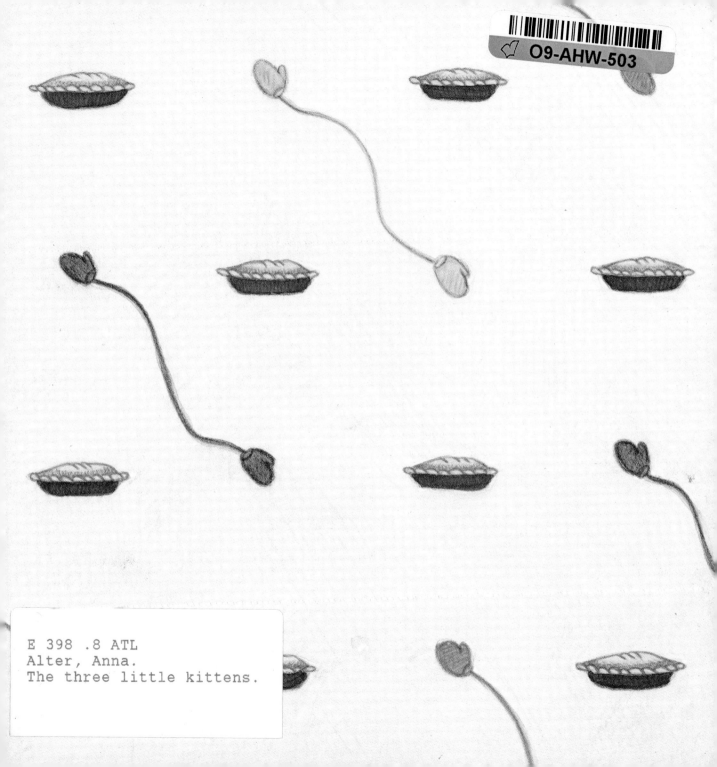

For my little thief

Henry Holt and Company, LLC, *Publishers since 1866*
115 West 18th Street, New York, New York 10011

Henry Holt is a registered trademark of Henry Holt and Company, LLC
Copyright © 2001 by Anna Alter. All rights reserved.
Published in Canada by Fitzhenry & Whiteside Ltd.,
195 Allstate Parkway, Markham, Ontario L3R 4T8.
Library of Congress Cataloging-in-Publication Data
The three little kittens / Anna Alter.
Summary: Three little kittens lose and find their mittens.
1. Nursery rhymes. 2. Children's poetry. [1. Nursery rhymes.] I. Alter, Anna.
PZ8.3T413 2001 398.8—dc21 [E] 00-57533
ISBN 0-8050-6471-0 / First Edition—2001 / Designed by Donna Mark
Printed in the United States of America on acid-free paper. ∞

The artist used watercolors and colored pencils on BFK Rives
printmaking paper to create the illustrations for this book.

1 3 5 7 9 10 8 6 4 2

The Three Little Kittens

Anna Alter

Henry Holt and Company . New York

The three little kittens

lost their mittens,

and they began to cry—

"Oh, Mother dear,
we sadly fear
our mittens we have lost."

"What! Lost your mittens—
you naughty kittens!
Then you shall have no pie."

Mee-ow, mee-ow, mee-ow,
mee-ow, mee-ow, mee-ow.

"Then we shall have no pie."

But the three little kittens
found their mittens,

and they began to cry—

"Oh, Mother dear,
see here, see here,
our mittens we have found!"

"What! Found your mittens—
you good little kittens."

"Then you shall have some pie!"
Purr-r, purr-r, purr-r,
purr-r, purr-r, purr-r.

"Then we shall have some pie!"

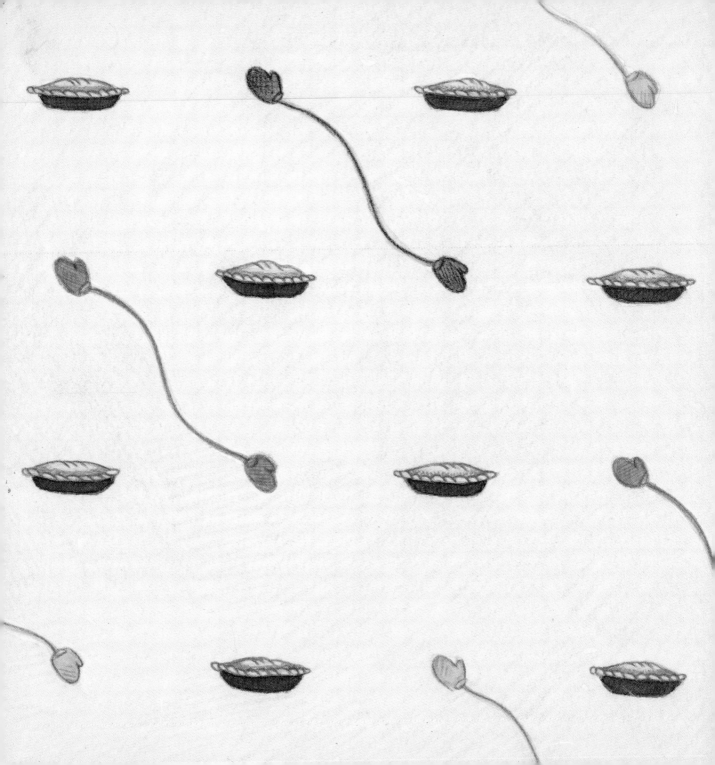